© 1994

School Zone Publishing
Grand Haven, MI

Library of Congress Cataloging-in-Publication Data

Vinje, Marie.
Cat That Sat, The / written by Marie Vinje ; ill. by Greta
Buchart.

Summary: A little boy tried to get his cat to move by rolling
the ball to him, bouncing the ball, and knocking things down
in his room – but the cat just sat.

ISBN: 0-88743-432-0 (paper)
1. Cats - fiction.
2. Easy reading.

CIP Data prepared by Medialog, Inc.

PREBOUND
LIBRARY
BOOKS

THE CAT THAT SAT

WRITTEN BY
MARIE VINJE

ILLUSTRATED BY
GRETA BUCHART

The cat just sat.

3

He would not play.

I rolled him the ball.

He looked away.

I bounced the ball.

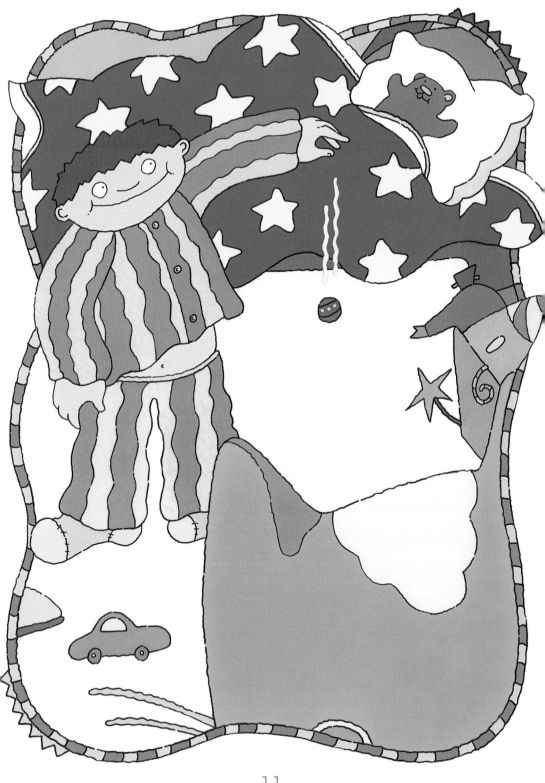

But the cat just sat.

The ball hit the wall.

Then it came back.

It bumped my blocks.

They began to fall.

The cat just sat.

23

He did not move at all!

My room is a mess.

What will Mother say?

And the cat just sat.

JUV
Vinj
The

Adult Book/Mend Disposition Slip
AGENCIES

To: (indicate below)

☐ Storage Services ☑ Technical Services
☐ Book Coordinator ☐ Reference

| Date: 7/8/2020 | Library LSMc | Initials |

Reason:

☑ Damaged/Worn Condition ☑ Discard

☐ Outdated

LAKE COUNTY PUBLIC LIBRARY
INDIANA

Pencil
+ crayon
marks.
Soiled

AD	FF	MU
AV	GR	NC
BO	HI	SJ
CL	HO	CN L
DS	LS	

JUL 2 6 '95

THIS BOOK IS RENEWABLE BY PHONE OR IN PERSON IF THERE IS NO RESERVE
WAITING OR FINE DUE.

LCP #0390